# The
# Ice Cream Scoop

At the ice cream parlor, Nancy, Bess, and George talked about their science report. Then the waitress brought Bess's sundae to the table.

Bess looked at the dish and smiled. It held one scoop of rich, golden brown peanut-butter-cup ice cream. Thick dark fudge with streaks of gooey marshmallow covered the top and ran down the sides.

Bess lifted up a heaping spoonful.

"Mmmm," she murmured, closing her eyes. She placed the spoon in her mouth.

Suddenly her eyes popped wide open. She gagged. She spit out the ice cream and shrieked, "I've been poisoned!"

# The Nancy Drew Notebooks

Available from MINSTREL Books

# THE
# NANCY DREW
## NOTEBOOKS®

#6

*The Ice Cream Scoop*

## CAROLYN KEENE
ILLUSTRATED BY ANTHONY ACCARDO

A MINSTREL® BOOK

Published by POCKET BOOKS
New York   London   Toronto   Sydney   Singapore

This book is a work of fiction. Names, characters, places, and incidents are products of the author's imagination or are used fictitiously. Any resemblance to actual events or locales or persons, living or dead, is entirely coincidental.

A MINSTREL PAPERBACK *ORIGINAL*

 A Minstrel Book published by
POCKET BOOKS, a division of Simon & Schuster Inc.
1230 Avenue of the Americas, New York, NY 10020

ISBN: 0-671-87950-2

First Minstrel Books printing May 1995

10  9  8  7  6  5

Cover art by Cliff Miller

Printed in the U.S.A.

# 1

# Sugar 'n' Spice

Nancy Drew glanced around Ms. Spencer's third-grade classroom. Suddenly she grinned. She leaned toward Bess Marvin's desk and whispered two words. "Ice cream."

Bess's eyes lit up. "Super idea!" she said. "Let's ask Ms. Spencer."

Nancy raised her hand as high as she could. Ms. Spencer nodded at her.

"May Bess, George, and I do our food report on ice cream?" Nancy asked. Bess Marvin and George Fayne—whose real name was Georgia—were Nancy's best friends.

Ms. Spencer didn't answer right away. She had been telling the class about a new science project. The students had divided themselves into teams. Each team would choose a favorite food and find out exactly what was in it. Then the teams would report on how the food was made and what nutrition it provided. No junk food was allowed.

Nancy held her breath. She really wanted to report on ice cream. Other teams had already picked tacos and pizza.

Finally Ms. Spencer said, "Well, ice cream does provide *some* nutrition. So I think I'll say yes."

George spun around in her seat and grinned at Nancy. "Way to go!" she whispered.

"Wait a minute," Ms. Spencer said. "We now have eight teams. Each team has three students, so that adds up to twenty-four. But there are twenty-five students in the class. Someone is missing from the list."

Jason Hutchings spoke up. "It's Mike Minelli. He went to the dentist."

"You're right," Ms. Spencer said. "We'll just add him to one of the teams. Does anyone know what he likes to eat?"

"He's an ice cream freak," Jason said.

"Uh-oh," Bess said, scrunching up her nose. She whispered to Nancy, "We don't want a *boy* on our team."

"No way!" Nancy said. She shook her head so hard that her long reddish blond hair swished back and forth.

"Ice cream it is," Ms. Spencer said. "We'll add Mike to that team."

"Phooey!" Bess muttered.

Nancy opened her mouth to say something, but just then the bell rang.

"That's the end of the school week," Ms. Spencer said. "I'll see you on Monday. And don't forget—food reports on Tuesday."

Nancy and Bess got their backpacks out of their cubbies. They waited for George outside the classroom.

"What a bummer!" Bess blurted out

as soon as George joined them. "We'd have so much more fun without Mike Minelli."

"I know," George said. "But at least we get to report on food we love."

"But what will we do when he starts to act gross?" Bess asked.

Nancy thought for a minute. Then she said, "I know what we should do right now. The three of us should start our research."

George didn't look happy. "Do you mean spend Friday afternoon at the library?"

Nancy laughed. "No, I mean ice cream research that's really fun."

"Like eating ice cream!" Bess said.

"Right," Nancy said. "Let's call home and ask permission."

The girls hurried to the public telephones in the school entry.

"I'll ask my mom if she can pick us up at Sugar 'n' Spice," George said as she looked for a coin in her backpack.

Sugar 'n' Spice was a small ice cream

shop. It had been in the neighborhood since long before the girls were born.

"Let's not go to Sugar 'n' Spice this time," Bess said. "For a change, let's go to the new place—the Double Dip."

"But Sugar 'n' Spice has the best ice cream," George said. "It's homemade."

"The Double Dip is so cute," said Bess. "It has those little tables and the striped awnings and matching chairs. There are more flavors at the Double Dip, too."

Nancy smiled. Sometimes it was hard to believe her two best friends were actually cousins. They were so different. George was tall with dark curly hair. She loved sports. Bess was shorter, had long blond hair, and liked clothes much more than outdoor games. And today the two girls even wanted to go to different ice cream places.

"Let's go to both," Nancy suggested. "First, Sugar 'n' Spice. Then we can try the Double Dip. They're only two blocks apart."

"Sounds scrumptious," Bess said.

As soon as they had permission, the girls walked to Sugar 'n' Spice. There were no other customers in the tiny shop when they arrived. The two wood tables, matching chairs, and big ceiling fan looked old-fashioned. But everything was scrubbed clean.

The three friends put their backpacks on a table. Under the glass counter was the refrigerator case. It held just six large plastic buckets of ice cream: vanilla, chocolate, strawberry, peach, coffee, and fudge ripple.

"Hi, Sid," Nancy said to the man behind the counter. Sid Alden owned Sugar 'n' Spice. With his white hair and big round belly, Nancy thought he looked just like Santa Claus without a beard.

Sid winked at the girls. "Nancy, George, and Bess. I haven't seen you in ages. It must be two days at least! Did you stop eating ice cream?"

The girls laughed. Nancy and George peered inside the refrigerator case.

"A chocolate cone for me," George said.

"I'll get that while Miss Drew makes up her mind between strawberry and fudge ripple," Sid said. "It won't take her more than two hours."

Everyone laughed again, although Nancy's cheeks turned pink. Strawberry and fudge ripple were her two favorite flavors. She always had trouble deciding which one to get.

"Last time I had fudge ripple," Nancy said. "So this time I'll get strawberry."

"And what about you, Bess?" Sid asked as he handed George her cone. "Two scoops, peach and chocolate, on a sugar cone?"

"Hmm," Bess murmured, staring at the buckets of smooth ice cream inside the case. "That *does* sound yummy." Without looking up, she finally sighed and said, "I still think I'll get ice cream at the Double Dip today."

Bess kept staring at the buckets of ice cream. But Nancy noticed that Sid

8

looked very angry. She had never seen him frown that way. He was holding her strawberry cone and glaring at Bess.

Suddenly Sid whacked the ice cream scoop against the metal edge of the counter.

"Why don't you kids just pay for your cones and get out of my shop!" he snapped. "And don't come back!"

# 2
# The Double Dip

**N**ancy couldn't believe what she'd just heard. She glanced at Bess. Bess looked as though she was about to cry.

"I'm sorry," Sid said right away. "Really sorry! I didn't mean that at all. You kids are terrific. It's just that the Double Dip is driving me out of business."

Sid handed Nancy her ice cream cone.

"Is Sugar 'n' Spice closing?" George gasped.

"*I* don't think so," someone said. The quiet voice came from behind Sid.

It was Bobby Alden, Sid's tall, thin grandson. He was fourteen and helped his grandfather after school almost every day.

Bobby stepped into the shop from the back room and gave his grandfather a hug. "Don't worry, Grandpa," he said. "Nothing bad will happen to Sugar 'n' Spice."

"I guess it's hard for me *not* to worry," Sid said. "Lots of people are going to the new place instead of coming here. There's more room to sit down at the Double Dip. And they have those crazy new flavors and toppings that people like—the ones that are full of candy. Our ice cream is plain and simple, but we use healthy natural ingredients."

"Your homemade ice cream is the best," Nancy said. Then she added, "We're doing a school report on how ice cream is made."

"Would you like me to show you?" Sid asked. "I'm making a new batch of peach on Sunday morning. You can come by and watch."

"That would be great!" Nancy said.

The girls paid for their ice cream and began walking up the street to the Double Dip.

"Yummy!" George said, licking her cone.

"Mmmm. Eeek!" Nancy yelped, trying to catch a drip that was running down her thumb.

"It would be terrible if Sugar 'n' Spice closed," Bess said. "Even if I want to go to the Double Dip once in a while, I love Sugar 'n' Spice."

Nancy nodded. "I wish both places could stay open."

"We could help," Bess suggested. "By eating twice as much ice cream."

"Good idea. Eeek!" Nancy yelped again as she tried to catch another drip.

George and Nancy finished their cones just as the girls got to the Double Dip. They stepped under the red, white, and green striped awning and opened the door.

"Hi," said a young woman with very short, curly brown hair. "Can I help you?"

"I'd like a sundae," Bess said.

"Isn't she pretty?" Nancy whispered to George. "She's Cathy Perez, the owner."

"Just follow me," Cathy said.

She led the girls to one of the small wooden tables next to a large window. Four red geranium plants sat on the windowsill. There was a fresh red rose in a little glass vase on each table.

"It's so pretty here," Bess said as she picked up the menu. "And I'm so hungry."

When the waiter came over, Bess ordered peanut-butter-cup ice cream with fudge sauce. "I'd better get the small size," she said. "It's before dinner."

"Oh, ick gross!" Nancy said.

Bess looked surprised. "What's wrong with peanut-butter-cup ice cream?" she asked.

Nancy laughed. "I wasn't talking about your ice cream," she explained. "I was talking about my hands. That strawberry cone dripped a lot. Now my hands stick to everything I touch. I'd better wash them."

Nancy walked to the back of the restaurant, to a short hallway. On the right was the door to the women's rest room.

When Nancy came out of the rest room, she noticed something. The door at the end of the hall was open.

What's in there? she wondered. She glanced around. No one was in sight. Just one little peek, Nancy thought. She quickly went to the door and stepped inside.

The room was medium size. Two huge stainless-steel freezers stood along one wall. They made a humming sound. Large jars of ice cream toppings, bottles of candy sprinkles, and other supplies lined some shelves. Along another wall stood a work table. High above the table was a small, open window. Stacks of empty plastic ice cream buckets stood on the floor.

It's just the storage room, Nancy thought. On the other side of the storage room was the back door to the shop. It was open.

Nancy turned to go, but her foot slipped. She stumbled against a stack of plastic buckets. They fell to the floor with a loud bang.

"I'd better pick these up," she said. But just as her fingers touched the plastic, someone behind her shouted, "Put those buckets down!"

# 3

# The Wrong Flavor

**N**ancy whirled around. Her heart was pounding. "I was just—" she started to say. But there was no one in the storage room.

Outside the back door, someone stepped into view. It was Cathy Perez. She was arguing with someone else. "You can't deliver that ice cream to my shop. I keep telling you—I didn't order it."

Nancy moved closer to see what was going on. A tan truck from the River Heights Dairy stood outside. A man was taking buckets of ice cream out of the truck and putting them on a delivery cart.

Cathy had her hands on her hips. "Ten buckets of pineapple–papaya crush ice cream? You've got to be kidding! That's my worst-selling flavor. I have exactly one customer who orders it."

The delivery man finished loading the buckets onto the cart. "Look, Miss," he said to Cathy. "I'm just doing my job. Here's the order form. It says, 'To the Double Dip.' "

Cathy stared at the form. "I never ordered this flavor," she insisted. "But the form does have my name on it." She sighed. "Okay. Load the ice cream into my freezer."

The delivery man pushed the cart into the storage room.

"This isn't your fault," Cathy said to him. "But I bet I know what happened. A high school girl was working for me. I had to fire her after two weeks. She was giving free ice cream to her friends. They gobbled up a lot of money. I bet she called in this phony order to get back at me."

Cathy saw Nancy standing near the door. "What are you doing here, honey?" she asked.

"I just got an idea," Nancy said. "I want to ask you about it. My friends and I are doing a school report on ice cream. Could you tell us about your new flavors? What goes into them? And what is popular?"

"I can tell you one thing right away," Cathy said. "Pineapple-papaya crush is *not* popular." Then she smiled at Nancy. "I would be glad to help you with your report. Why don't all of you stop by tomorrow at four o'clock?"

Nancy thanked Cathy and started to hurry back to her friends. She ran into George near the rest room.

"What took so long?" George asked. "You must have the world's cleanest hands."

"I was just poking around," Nancy said.

When they got back to the table, Bess said, "There you are! I was saving you a taste of my sundae, Nancy. But it started to melt. So . . ."

Nancy looked at Bess's dish and laughed. There wasn't a drop of ice cream left in it.

George glanced at the clock on the wall. "Let's get going," she said. "We can wait for my mom outside."

Bess paid for her sundae, and the girls went outside. While they waited, Nancy took a purple pen and a small notebook with a shiny blue cover out of her backpack.

"Nancy!" George said. "Do you have a new mystery? Why didn't you tell us?"

Nancy loved to solve mysteries, and she was good at it. Her father had given her the blue notebook so that she could write down clues and suspects. When Nancy took out her notebook, her best friends knew there might be a case to solve.

Nancy told the girls about Cathy Perez and the strange ice cream delivery.

"I'm not sure it's a mystery," Nancy said. "But I'd better write everything down. Just in case."

On one notebook page Nancy wrote: "10 gallons pineapple-papaya crush. To the Double Dip. Who ordered it?" At the top of the next page, she wrote: "Suspects." Below that she wrote: "Girl fired by Cathy Perez."

Then Nancy said to her friends, "I asked Cathy to help us with our report. She said we can talk to her tomorrow. Is that okay?"

"Sure," George said. "We should go to the library, too. It's not open on Sunday."

Nancy nodded. "I'll call Mike Minelli tonight and ask if he can meet us."

"Hey, you just saved a telephone call," Bess said. "Look who's sitting in that car."

A bright red car had pulled up in front of the Double Dip. A boy wearing a baseball cap backward sat in the backseat. When he saw the girls, he grinned. Then he pressed his face against the car window until it looked like a yellowish pink pancake.

"Oooooooh," Bess moaned. "What did I tell you? Mike Minelli is gross!"

The three friends went over to the car. Mike's seventeen-year-old brother was sitting in the driver's seat. A girl with spiky black hair sat next to him. When Mike rolled down the car window, Nancy told him about the food report.

"With the three of you!" Mike yelled. "How did I get on a girls' team?"

"Jason Hutchings told Ms. Spencer you're an ice cream freak," Bess explained.

"Gee, thanks a heap, Jason," Mike muttered.

"We're meeting at the public library tomorrow," Nancy said. "So if you want to work with us—"

Mike's brother leaned across the seat. "Donna and I have to go to the library in the morning," he said to Mike. "We

22

can take you." Then he nodded to the girls and added, "I'm Carl. This is my girlfriend, Donna Kepler."

A few seconds later a green car pulled up behind Carl's car.

"There's my mom," George said.

The third graders made plans to meet at the library at ten o'clock. Everyone said goodbye. Mrs. Fayne drove the girls home.

After dinner that evening Nancy played a five-game domino tournament with her father. Carson Drew was a famous lawyer, but Nancy often beat him at dominoes. While they played, Nancy told him everything that had happened.

"Strawberry, chocolate, and peanut-butter-cup ice cream today," said Carson Drew. "New flavors tomorrow. Peach on Sunday. You kids are going to turn into ice cream! What flavor will you be?"

"Pumpkin!" Nancy answered. Pumpkin was one of Carson Drew's nicknames for Nancy.

Mr. Drew laughed and said, "Speaking of pumpkins, you really will turn into one if you don't get ready for bed!"

The next morning Nancy got up and put on jeans and a new turquoise sweatshirt. After breakfast Hannah Gruen drove her to the library. Hannah was the Drew family's housekeeper. She usually had Saturday morning off. But that morning Nancy's father had work to do in the office.

Hannah had lived with the Drews since Nancy was three years old and her mother had died. Since then Hannah had been like a mother to Nancy.

Nancy met George and Bess in the lobby of the library. They went to the reference room. The encyclopedias were kept there. Mike Minelli was already sitting at a long wooden table. He was reading a big encyclopedia for kids.

"This is great stuff!" Mike said when he saw them. "Want to hear about icebergs and ice hockey? Or ice picks and ice axes?"

"How about ice cream?" George asked. "Remember the report we have to do?"

"What report?" Mike asked. Then he burst out laughing. "Just kidding," he said.

Bess rolled her eyes and groaned.

A librarian helped them find another encyclopedia and a book about dairies. Then the team began to read and take notes.

"Most ice cream is made from cream, sugar, and different flavorings," Mike said.

"You can add fresh fruit," George said. "But this book says you have to soak the fruit in sugar and water first. That keeps it from freezing completely."

"Look at this," Bess said. "It's a picture of a big ice cream maker. It's the kind dairies and restaurants use."

"That's pretty neat," Nancy said. "Let's make a copy of it for our report."

Nancy carried the encyclopedia to a

copy machine in the copy room. As she put a coin in the slot, someone said, "Hey, aren't you one of the ice cream kids?"

Nancy turned around. An older girl with spiky black hair was standing behind her. It was Donna Kepler, Carl Minelli's girlfriend.

"How's the report going?" Donna asked.

"We found some good information here," Nancy said. "And this afternoon we're going to the Double Dip to talk to the owner."

"Cathy Perez!" Donna said. "Don't mention that woman or the Double Dip around me. I used to work there. Cathy fired me. Now I hate the Double Dip. I'd love to see that place close down!"

# 4

# Two New Suspects

**N**ancy's blue eyes opened wide. She swallowed hard and tried to think of something to say. But before she did, Donna started to walk away. "See you later," Donna called over her shoulder.

Yipes! Nancy thought. Donna Kepler is the girl who was fired! Did she call in the phony order for pineapple–papaya crush ice cream? Is the phony order part of a plan to make Cathy close down the Double Dip?

Nancy finished copying the picture and rushed back to the reference room. She wanted to tell Bess and George what she'd found out.

"Uh-oh," she murmured when she

saw her friends. Carl Minelli and Donna Kepler were at their table.

"We finished taking notes," Bess said. "I'm going to call my mom to tell her she doesn't have to pick us up. Carl says he'll drive us." Mrs. Marvin had invited Nancy and George for lunch.

"Let's get out of here," Mike said. "It's not good for your health to spend too much time in a library on Saturday. I read that in one of these encyclopedias."

"Under *H* for *health?*" George asked with a grin. "Or *S* for *Saturday?*"

Bess called her mother. Then Carl drove the girls to Bess's house.

"See you at four," Nancy said to Mike.

Mrs. Marvin made tomato soup and grilled cheese sandwiches for lunch. The girls set the kitchen table. As soon as they sat down to eat, Nancy told her friends about Donna Kepler.

"What Donna said was mean!" Bess exclaimed. "Could she really do something to make Cathy close the Double Dip?"

"It would have to be something bigger than a phony ice cream order," George said.

Nancy nodded. "But remember, we don't have proof yet that Donna did anything."

Nancy got her pen and blue notebook out of her backpack. On the page labeled "Suspects" she wrote: "Donna Kepler wants the Double Dip to close."

After lunch the girls went up to the attic. Mrs. Marvin kept a big trunk of old clothes there. They were perfect for playing dress-up. Bess and Nancy pretended they were movie stars. George was a TV reporter who asked them questions.

At a quarter to four the girls put the clothes away and hurried to the Double Dip. A few minutes later Mike met them inside.

"Yo, team!" Mike said. "I made up a cheer for us. Listen. Two, four, six, eight. Bugs on ice cream sure taste great!"

"Grosser than gross," Bess muttered.

"There's Cathy," George said. She pointed to the back of the restaurant.

Nancy waved. The owner of the Double Dip smiled and motioned them to come over.

"How about a quick look at the freezers?" Cathy asked. "Then I'll show you all the flavors in the refrigerator case."

The children followed Cathy to the storage room. They gathered around one of the tall stainless-steel freezers. The door opened like a refrigerator door. Inside were rows of large plastic buckets of ice cream.

"To make things easy to find, I keep the smooth flavors, like plain chocolate, in here," Cathy said. "And fruit sherbets, too."

"All the buckets have the same kind of label," Nancy said.

"That's right," Cathy said. "I get all my ice cream from the River Heights Dairy."

Then she opened the second freezer. "I store the ice creams with nuts, fruit, and candy in here."

"Will the dairy make any flavor you want?" Mike asked. "Like pickle chip with ketchup ripples?"

"Super sicko!" Bess whispered to Nancy.

Cathy laughed. "No, but the dairy offers quite a variety of flavors.

"Br-r-r-r." George shivered. "How cold is it in there?"

"Zero degrees Fahrenheit," Cathy said. She shut the freezer door. "This ice cream is too hard to scoop out. It softens when we move it to the refrigerator case. We keep the case at thirty degrees Fahrenheit."

"What do you do if the ice cream gets too soft?" Mike asked.

"You should never let that happen," Cathy said. "Refrozen ice cream isn't as smooth. Sometimes it tastes funny, too."

Cathy took the children back to the

restaurant. A long counter ran along the wall near the refrigerator case. The sundaes and sodas were made there. Cathy also showed them the milk shake blender.

"Where's Mike?" George asked.

Everyone glanced around. Mike was nowhere to be seen. A minute later he walked out of the men's rest room.

"Did I miss any free samples?" he asked.

Cathy smiled and shook her head. "I was about to show you the most popular flavors."

Just then a phone rang. Cathy stepped into the little room that was her office. A minute later she leaned out the door.

"I'm sorry," she said. "I have to go over some important business on the phone. Can we finish the tour some other time?"

The ice cream team said yes. Cathy waved goodbye and went back into her office. Mike and the girls walked outside.

"See you later, alligators," Mike said.

"Don't forget," George said. "Ten o'clock tomorrow at Sugar 'n' Spice."

"Too bad they're making peach ice cream," Mike said as he walked away. "Instead of something good—like meatball!"

That evening Nancy and her father ate dinner earlier than usual. They wanted to see a seven-thirty movie at the neighborhood theater. A new comedy about a Little League baseball team was playing.

After they washed the dishes, Nancy changed clothes. She put on a light green corduroy jumper and a white turtleneck shirt.

Mr. Drew drove to the theater. But by the time they arrived, the parking lot was full. They finally found a place to park across the street from the Double Dip.

When the show was over, Nancy and

her father strolled back to the car. They loved to talk about the movies they saw together. Near the Double Dip, they ran into Mr. and Mrs. Minelli and Mike. They were all eating ice-cream cones.

"Hello there," Mr. Drew said. Then he grinned at Mike. "Didn't you get tired of ice cream today?"

Mike shook his head. "Learning about it isn't the same as eating it," he said. "And I had super luck at the Double Dip tonight. My favorite flavor is on sale for half price."

"What flavor?" Nancy asked.

Mike held up his cone. "Pineapple-papaya crush!"

# 5
# Pineapple-Papaya Crush

**N**ancy gulped. The one customer who ordered pineapple-papaya crush at the Double Dip was Mike Minelli!

Her mind began to race. Was this just a coincidence? Or did it mean something?

Nancy stared at the two fat scoops of ice cream. They were yellowish white with chunks of bright yellow and pinkish orange. Her stomach did a flip-flop. Pineapple-papaya crush looks awful, she thought. It figures that Mike would like it!

Everyone was saying goodbye. Nancy could only nod. She was quiet during the ride home, too. Carson Drew ruffled her hair and said, "Tired, Pumpkin Ice Cream? We'll be home in a minute."

Nancy usually told her father everything. When she had a mystery to solve, he made good suggestions. But that night she wasn't ready to talk. She needed some time to figure things out.

Nancy brushed her teeth as fast as she could. Then she put on her pink-checked pajamas and got into bed. She opened her notebook and read what she had written:

"10 gallons pineapple-papaya crush. To the Double Dip. Who ordered it?"

Nancy began to ask herself questions. Does Mike Minelli have something to do with the phony ice cream order? Is he trying to help his brother's girlfriend get back at Cathy Perez? Did he guess that Cathy would put his favorite ice cream on sale?

Nancy wrote these questions on the same page. Then she turned out the light. She tried to sleep, but more ice cream worries kept popping into her mind.

Would other strange things happen at the Double Dip? Would Donna Kepler find a way to close down the shop? Suppose Sugar 'n' Spice and the Double Dip both went out of business! Two nice people would lose their shops. The neighborhood would have no ice cream place!

Nancy tossed and turned. Thinking about ice cream was giving her a headache. She was afraid she would never fall asleep. But a few minutes later, she did. The next thing she knew, it was Sunday morning. Sunlight was streaming through her bedroom window.

Nancy jumped out of bed and washed up. She knew it would be fun to watch Sid Alden make his delicious ice cream. She put on her red, long-sleeved Sandburg Elementary School T-shirt and jeans. She ran downstairs to the kitchen. Hannah was making waffles.

After breakfast with her father, Nancy had time to read the Sunday comics. Then she rode her bike to

Sugar 'n' Spice. When she got there, Mike Minelli was locking up his bike. Bess and George arrived a minute later.

The shop didn't open for customers until noon. Bess knocked on the door. Bobby Alden let them in and took them to the back room.

"Here it is," Sid said, grinning. "The machine that makes the great stuff you eat!"

He pointed to something that looked like a narrow, stainless-steel washing machine. It had a round door on the front. On the top was a shallow sink and water spigot.

Sid opened the door. Nancy and the others crowded around. They saw a large cylinder inside. Round steel blades spiraled down the middle of the cylinder.

"Wow," Bess said. "It's so shiny."

"You bet," Sid said. "We sterilize it with a special cleaner before we use it."

Sid handed Bobby a big plastic jug. "You start the show," he said.

Bobby poured thick white cream from the jug into the top of the machine. "This special cream from the dairy has sugar in it," he said.

Sid picked up a large bowl of peeled, sliced peaches. He handed Nancy a scoop. "Into the hopper," he said. He pointed to a small boxlike opening on the machine's door.

Nancy carefully scooped all the peaches into the hopper.

"Nice job," Bobby said. "I usually drop a few." Then he handed Mike a brown glass bottle. "Empty what's left into the hopper."

Mike sniffed the bottle. "Smells like shoe polish, boiled cabbage, and rotten cheese."

George sniffed the bottle, too. "It does not! It smells like peaches."

"It's peach extract," Sid said. "Made from real peaches. It gives the ice cream more flavor. I never use those artificial extracts, even though they're cheaper."

Mike poured the extract into the hopper.

"Ready for blastoff?" Sid asked. "Press that switch to the right, Bess."

Bess pressed a switch on the front of the machine. The motor began to whir.

"What's going on in there?" Nancy asked.

"Well," Sid said, "the cylinder gets very cold. So a thin layer of cream freezes on it. The blades turn all the time. They scrape off the frozen cream. At the same time they push more liquid cream against the cold cylinder. Pretty soon there's no more liquid. The cream is all whipped up."

"How soon is pretty soon?" Mike asked.

"Fifteen or twenty minutes," Sid said.

While they waited, Sid let the kids sniff bottles of vanilla and strawberry extract. He showed them the containers of chocolate fudge.

"What would happen if you put a lot of salt in the hopper?" Mike asked.

"Why would anyone do that?" Sid asked.

"You might get ice cream that tastes good with potato chips," Mike said.

Sid shook his head. "I'd lose all my customers and be out of business in a flash."

Bess sighed and muttered to Nancy, "Mike Minelli must have been born really weird."

Sid took a second bowl of peaches out of the refrigerator. "Just a minute to go," he said. "Get those into the machine, George."

George put the fruit into the hopper.

"These peaches won't be inside long enough to be chopped up completely," Sid said. "That's how we get the little peach chunks that Bess likes so much."

Sid uncovered a round opening in the door. Bobby put a plastic bucket under it. Then he pressed the switch to the left.

"What's happening?" Nancy asked.

"The blades are turning in the opposite direction now," Bobby explained. "They'll push out the ice cream."

"Here it comes!" Bess exclaimed.

"Oops! I think you used the wrong recipe," Mike said. "That's not ice cream."

The children bent over the bucket.

"It looks like peach-colored whipped cream," George said. "Only heavier."

Sid chuckled as he snapped a lid on the bucket. "Now it goes into the flash freezer. Fifty degrees below zero finishes the job."

"You mean no one gets to try it?" Bess asked. She looked very disappointed.

"Not for six hours," Sid said. "How about a taste of the batch I made earlier instead?"

Bobby gave everyone a small dish of peach ice cream.

"Dee-lish!" Mike said as he ate. "Now I know what I want to be when I grow up."

Nancy's eyes twinkled. She leaned toward Mike and said, "An ice cream bucket!"

Everyone laughed, even Mike.

"This has been fun," Sid said. "The shop hasn't been this lively in weeks."

Before leaving, the kids thanked Sid and Bobby for everything. When they were outside, George said, "We should finish talking to Cathy Perez this afternoon."

"You'll have to go without me," Mike said. "I'm playing miniature golf. With boys!"

The girls made plans to meet again at four o'clock. Nancy rode home. After lunch Carson Drew helped her practice skating on her new in-line skates. Before she knew it, it was time to bike to the Double Dip.

Nancy, Bess, and George met inside the restaurant. They gathered around the refrigerator case. Cathy Perez began showing them the twenty flavors inside.

"I'll have to hurry," Cathy said. "Just four people work here. Ray does dishes and cleanup. Tom and my cousin Meg wait on tables. And I do everything else."

She pointed to a tub of very dark brown ice cream. "Fudge-nut brownie is popular," she said. "And so is coffee-toffee crunch."

Suddenly a frightened screech cut through the air. "H-E-E-L-P!"

Cathy dropped the ice cream scoop that she was holding. The screech was followed by a loud thud. And then another thud.

Cathy gasped. "The storage room!"

# 6

# Chocolate Melt

Cathy dashed off without another word. The girls raced after her. They all burst into the storage room—and stopped short.

"Meg!" Cathy exclaimed. "Are you all right?"

The young waitress was standing in front of a freezer. Its door was open. Two ice cream buckets were lying on the floor. Their lids had fallen off. There were big splashes of melted chocolate ice cream all over.

"I was getting a bucket from the top shelf," Meg said. Her voice sounded shaky. "Everything was slippery and wet and squishy. When one bucket slipped out of my hands, I knocked over another one."

"The important thing is that you're not hurt," Cathy said. "But I don't understand why this chocolate ice cream is so soft."

Meg's face looked pale. "It's not just this chocolate," she said. "Everything in the freezer is melted."

"Melted!" Cathy said. She hurried to the freezer and examined the ice cream.

Nancy moved closer. The buckets looked moist. Water dripped from the shelves.

"Did someone turn off the freezer?" Cathy asked. She checked the on-off switch. "It's still on," she said. "Maybe it's the electricity." She knelt down to look behind the freezer. When she stood up, the heavy electrical cord was dangling from her hand.

"Somebody unplugged this freezer!" she said. She looked at the dripping shelves. "An entire supply of ice cream—ruined! First the pineapple–papaya crush. Now this!"

Cathy began emptying the freezer. "Someone must have sneaked in yesterday," she said. "We wouldn't have noticed any change in the ice cream for a while. Then the freezer was off all night."

"I don't remember seeing anyone around here," Meg said. "But we're all so busy."

"Uh-oh," Nancy murmured. "This is bad."

"What's bad?" George asked. "Nancy, what's wrong? You look really strange!"

"I think I just figured out something very creepy," Nancy whispered.

"Tell us," George said.

"Tell us while we get a snack," Bess said. "Creepy makes me hungry."

The girls sat at one of the restaurant tables. Meg came to take their order.

"A cherry soda with vanilla ice cream, please," Bess said.

"A root beer float for me," George said.

"I'll have a dish of chocolate ripple ice cream," Nancy said. "I mean, make that strawberry. Or maybe—" Nancy took a deep breath. "One scoop of each, please."

"Now tell us everything," Bess said.

"When I was looking at that melted ice cream, I remembered two things," Nancy began. "They both happened yesterday—when we were all here. First, Mike asked Cathy about ice cream getting too soft."

George nodded. "Cathy said refrozen ice cream isn't smooth."

"Right," Nancy said. "Then we left the storage room, and he disappeared."

"He was in the rest room," Bess said.

"But suppose he was in the rest room just part of the time," Nancy said.

Meg appeared carrying a tray. She put spoons, straws, napkins, and the ice cream dishes on the table. The girls thanked her.

George was staring at Nancy. "You think Mike Minelli unplugged the freezer!"

Nancy told her friends about Mike and the pineapple–papaya crush ice cream. "I thought it might be a coincidence," Nancy said. "But now I think he's helping Donna Kepler close down this place."

"This *is* creepy!" George said.

Bess nodded. "Mike Minelli is pretty gross and sort of weird," she said. "But I never thought he was . . ." Her voice died away. She looked sad. She put a straw in her soda and sipped very slowly.

For the first time ever, the three friends ate their ice cream in silence. Nancy wrote everything in her notebook. On the page labeled Suspects she added the name *Mike Minelli*.

That evening Nancy ate dinner with her father. She filled him in on the mystery.

"I know the Minelli family," Carson Drew said. "It's hard to understand Mike being involved in something like this. But you discovered some troubling clues."

Nancy's father twirled a few strands of spaghetti around his fork. Then he asked, "Besides Donna Kepler, who has a reason to hurt the Double Dip?"

Nancy thought about that, then answered, "Well . . . Sid Alden. He says the Double Dip is driving Sugar 'n' Spice out of business. He could have called in the phony ice cream order. But how could he have pulled the freezer plug?"

The more Nancy thought about it, the more upset she felt. "I can't believe Sid would do anything bad," she said. "I just can't."

After dinner Nancy started a chart for the science report. It showed how to make peach ice cream. George was writing about the ice cream maker. Mike was reporting on nutrition. Bess was doing flavors.

Before going to bed, Nancy got out her blue notebook. She placed it on the desk unopened. She tapped her purple pen on the cover. Tap-tap. Tap-tap. Finally she opened to the page labeled Suspects. Under Mike Minelli's name she wrote, "Sid Alden."

Nancy climbed into bed and turned out the bedside lamp. But her eyes stayed open. She whispered, "If Mike or Sid is behind this, I want to know. And I want to know as soon as possible!"

The next day school went by slowly for Nancy. She looked at the clock again and again. Ten-thirty. Noon. Two-fifteen.

I need more clues, she thought. But what? And where?

Finally the afternoon bell rang.

"Don't forget," Ms. Spencer said. "Food reports tomorrow morning. All the teams should be ready."

Nancy, Bess, and George hurried to get their backpacks out of their cubbies. Mike Minelli came up to them, waving some papers.

"Yo, team!" he said. "I finished my part of the report. So I get to watch a tape with Carl and Donna tonight. *Galactic Hero!*"

Mike sprinted down the hall to catch up with Jason. The girls headed for the exit.

"Guess what I dreamed last night," Bess said. "I was in math class. But I was eating a peanut-butter-cup sundae with hot marshmallow fudge. Mmmm! Let's get one."

George scrunched up her nose and glanced at Nancy. The two girls did not look eager.

Nancy sighed. "I think I've had enough ice cream for a while."

"Ditto," George said.

"Come with me and just keep me company," Bess said.

The girls called home for permission. Then they walked to the Double Dip.

When they got to the restaurant, Cathy waved to them. "Hi," she said. "What's on your menu for today? Looking or eating?"

"I'm eating," Bess said. "Nancy and George are looking—at me."

When the girls were seated, Meg took Bess's order. She came back a minute later and said, "The hot marshmallow fudge container is empty. There's more marshmallow fudge in the storage room. But it will take a little while to heat up."

While Bess waited, the girls talked about their science report. Then Meg brought Bess's sundae to the table.

Bess looked at the dish and smiled. It held one scoop of rich, golden brown peanut-butter-cup ice cream. Thick dark fudge with streaks of gooey marshmallow covered the top and ran down the sides. Bess lifted up a heaping spoonful.

"Mmmm," she murmured, closing her eyes. She placed the spoon in her mouth.

Suddenly her eyes popped wide open. She gagged. She spit out the ice cream and shrieked, "I've been poisoned!"

# 7

# Don't Eat the Ice Cream

Everyone in the restaurant turned and stared at Bess. Cathy and Meg rushed over.

"What's going on?" Cathy asked.

Bess held one hand over her mouth. With the other she pointed to her sundae. Cathy bent down and sniffed the ice cream. Then she tasted a tiny bit of marshmallow fudge.

"Ugh!" she said. "It's full of salt!"

Salt! Nancy thought. It's Mike Minelli again. He asked Sid about putting salt in ice cream!

Cathy had Bess rinse out her mouth and then drink some water. Meg explained that she had used a new jar of fudge from the storage room.

"I want to see that fudge," Cathy said.

The girls followed Cathy to the counter where the sundaes were made.

"Someone stirred a lot of salt into this fudge," Cathy muttered. "I'd better check everything in the storage room."

Meg and the girls went with Cathy. She opened the door with a key.

"Here's where I got the jar," Meg said. She pointed to the middle of one shelf.

Cathy sampled all the other jars of fudge. They were fine. Everything else on the shelves was all right, too.

"Hey, look at this," Nancy said. "Fingerprints!" She had found fudge smudges on the edge of the shelf.

"How did anyone get in here again?" Cathy asked angrily. "We open the back door only for deliveries. Or to put out garbage. I started locking the inside door. Meg and I have the only keys."

Nancy looked around. "What about that window?" she asked. She pointed to the small open window high above the table.

"It's for ventilation," Cathy said. "But who could get in it? It's so narrow and high up. Well, I'll shut it from now on.'"

Cathy turned to Bess and said, "Let's get you a new sundae—on the house."

"Well, uh—" Bess stammered. "For once I don't feel like ice cream."

The girls said goodbye to Cathy and Meg. Outside the restaurant Nancy asked, "Do you remember this? Mike Minelli talked about putting salt in ice cream."

"That's right!" George said.

"Yuck," Bess said. "I never thought ice cream would seem so creepy."

The girls talked for a few minutes. Then Nancy said, "I'd better get home. I want to finish my ice cream chart."

Bess and George waved goodbye. Nancy started up the block. The mystery was on her mind. When she got to the corner, she suddenly turned around.

I'll take a quick look behind the Double Dip, she thought. Maybe I'll find a clue.

She hurried to the back of the shop. A large garbage pail stood below the storage room window. The top was half off.

Maybe Mike stood on that pail to reach the window, Nancy thought. But he still would be too short. She stepped closer. Could Donna fit through that window? she asked herself. I don't think so.

Nancy wrinkled up her nose. The garbage was smelly. She glanced down. A brown glass bottle was lying on top of the garbage.

That looks familiar, Nancy thought.

The bottle wasn't dirty, so Nancy picked it up carefully. She read the label.

"Natural peach extract!" she exclaimed. "This is from Sugar 'n' Spice. It's Sid's!"

Then Nancy noticed white specks around the bottle opening. "Salt!"

She got out her blue notebook and turned to the list of suspects. She circled a name: Sid Alden. Then she stared at the window.

Nancy slammed her notebook shut. She stuffed it and the bottle into her backpack. Then she started to run as fast as she could.

Three minutes later Nancy burst into Sugar 'n' Spice. She was breathing hard.

"Whoa!" Sid said. "Why all the running? The ice cream isn't going anywhere."

Nancy opened her backpack. She spoke between pants. "I've—got—to see—Bobby."

"He's working in back," Sid said.

Nancy rushed into the back room. Bobby was shutting the freezer door. He turned around.

Nancy glanced at his jeans. Then she set the brown bottle on a table and said, *"You're* the one who's trying to close down the Double Dip!"

# 8

# Nancy's Fudge Berry Clue

**B**obby's eyes grew round. His thin shoulders trembled.

"You called in that phony order of pineapple–papaya crush ice cream," Nancy said. "You unplugged Cathy's freezer. And you put salt in her hot marshmallow fudge!"

Bobby opened his mouth but didn't speak. His eyes shifted to something behind Nancy.

"I'd like to know what's going on."

Nancy jumped at the sound of the voice. Sid was standing behind her.

Bobby's eyes filled with tears. "I

wanted to save Sugar 'n' Spice, Grandpa," he said. "You've worked so hard your whole life. So I tried to hurt the Double Dip. I know I shouldn't have done it. I wish I hadn't. I really wish I hadn't!"

Sid sat down on a stool. His face was sad. "Tell me what you did," he said.

"I knew Cathy Perez got her ice cream from the River Heights Dairy. And I knew that pineapple–papaya crush isn't popular. So I phoned in an order for ten gallons."

Sid looked even sadder.

Bobby went on. "On Saturday I passed by the Double Dip. A big delivery had just arrived. I sneaked in the back door and unplugged a freezer. That's when I noticed the open window."

"What open window?" Sid asked.

"A little window in the storage room," Bobby said. He had to take a deep breath before he could go on. "This morning I got up early. I filled an empty bottle with salt. Then I climbed through the window and stirred the salt into a new jar of marshmallow fudge."

Bobby sank down on a stool. He covered his face with his hands.

"Everything you did was wrong, Bobby," Sid said. "So you ended up hurting everyone. You hurt Cathy Perez, yourself, and me."

"I know," Bobby whispered. After a minute he looked up and said to Sid, "We should go to the Double Dip now. I want to tell Cathy Perez everything."

Sid, Bobby, and Nancy left the shop. Sid hung a sign on the door. It said Closed. Then he locked the door.

Just before Nancy turned to go, Sid patted her on the head. She and Bobby looked at each other. He didn't look angry.

Nancy got home at the same time as her father. She asked if they could go into his study. Then she told him the whole story.

"Pumpkin, you did fine detective work," Carson Drew said. "I'm proud of you. Now let's hope that Bobby, Sid, and Cathy can work things out."

After dinner Nancy had to finish her ice cream chart. But she took a minute to phone Bess and George.

"Meet me at school tomorrow ten minutes early," Nancy said. "I have big news."

The next morning Hannah drove Nancy to the school entrance. George and Bess hurried up the front walk.

"Tell us everything," Bess said. "I can't believe you made us wait all night!"

"I solved the mystery," Nancy said. Then she told her friends what happened.

"How did you guess it was Bobby and not Mike or Sid?" George asked.

"The window was too high for Mike Minelli," Nancy answered. "It was too small for Sid. Then I remembered something. Bobby heard Mike talk about putting salt in ice cream. That gave Bobby the idea. When I got to Sugar 'n' Spice, I knew I was right."

"How?" George asked.

"Bobby had marshmallow fudge smudges on his jeans," Nancy explained. "Sid doesn't use marshmallow fudge. Only plain fudge."

"Wow!" Bess said. "You are the best!"

The girls entered the building with the other children. They put their sweaters, jackets, and backpacks in their cubbies.

"The good news is this," Bess said. "The Double Dip won't close."

"But we don't know what will happen to Sugar 'n' Spice," George added.

Nancy shook her head. "Not yet."

Mike Minelli ran by. "Go team!" he called out. Then he stopped and asked, "What kind of ice cream does the Galactic Hero eat?" He answered the riddle himself. "Computer chip!" and burst out laughing. "Get it? The Galactic Hero is an android!"

Mike went into the classroom doubled over with laughter. The girls couldn't help smiling.

"It's nice to know he's *only* gross and weird," Bess said.

The school day began with math review and new math problems. Then there was reading aloud from *The Wonderful Wizard of Oz*. At ten-thirty Ms. Spencer asked the students to take out their food reports.

"Each team will tell us about its food," she explained. "Then I'll collect the written reports."

Ms. Spencer's eyes twinkled. "Shall we hear about ice cream first?" she asked.

"I scream for ice cream!" Jason said.

Everyone laughed and clapped. The ice cream team walked to the front of the room.

"You're on," Bess whispered to Nancy.

Nancy held up her chart and took a deep breath. "Here's the scoop on ice cream."

69

She didn't get to say another word. The door swung open. Two people walked in.

"It's Cathy Perez and Sid Alden," George whispered. "And look what Sid has!"

Sid was carrying a large ice cream bucket. He put it on Ms. Spencer's desk.

"Class," Ms. Spencer said, "these are the owners of the Double Dip and Sugar 'n' Spice. They've planned a surprise for you."

Cathy laughed and said, "We gave the ice cream team lots of information. But we think their report needs some real ice cream."

"We have some neighborhood news, too," Sid said. "The Double Dip and Sugar 'n' Spice are joining together. I'll be making all the ice cream for the Double Dip. I'll make my usual flavors—but get ready for some new ones."

Cathy nodded. "In fact, get ready

right now. To celebrate our partnership, we've already created something new. I hope you like it."

Ms. Spencer passed out plastic dishes and spoons. Sid and Cathy scooped out ice cream. When they got to Nancy, they stopped for a minute.

"Thanks for your detective work," Sid said. "You stopped a lot of trouble."

"Sid and I had a long talk yesterday," Cathy said. "We realized we could help each other by making one business. We'll have the best ice cream in town—"

"In the prettiest restaurant," Sid said. "But I'll keep making the ice cream in my old shop. I'll sell take-out there, too."

Nancy was thrilled. "It's perfect!" Then she asked, "What about Bobby?"

"He'll have to pay for all the melted ice cream and the pineapple-papaya crush," Sid said. "It will take him a long time to earn that money."

"He understands how wrong he was," Cathy added. "He's learning the real way to help."

"Now enjoy your ice cream," Sid said.

Nancy looked in her bowl. She saw a scoop of pink ice cream with dark brown streaks. She tasted a spoonful.

"Fresh strawberry with fudge ripples. It's my dream ice cream come true," she said.

"My dream has come true, too," Bess said. "Eating ice cream in class!"

"Yeah, this stuff is good," Mike Minelli said. "Almost as good as pineapple-papaya crush. What's it called?"

Sid and Cathy answered together. "Nancy's Fudge Berry Clue!"

Nancy smiled and took out her blue notebook. She ate her ice cream slowly while she wrote.

I solved the mystery—and a lot of ice cream problems, too. Sid won't lose his business. Cathy won't lose hers. And we'll all have the perfect ice cream place. But here's the real scoop: I learned that you can't ever help someone by hurting someone else. Case closed.